Dear Parent:

Congratulations! Your child is taking the first steps on an exciting journey. The destination? Independent reading!

STEP INTO READING® will help your child get there. The program offers five steps to reading success. Each step includes fun stories and colorful art. There are also Step into Reading Sticker Books, Step into Reading Math Readers, Step into Reading Phonics Readers, Step into Reading Write-In Readers, and Step into Reading Phonics Boxed Sets—a complete literacy program with something to interest every child.

Learning to Read, Step by Step!

Ready to Read   Preschool–Kindergarten
• big type and easy words • rhyme and rhythm • picture clues
For children who know the alphabet and are eager to begin reading.

Reading with Help   Preschool–Grade 1
• basic vocabulary • short sentences • simple stories
For children who recognize familiar words and sound out new words with help.

Reading on Your Own   Grades 1–3
• engaging characters • easy-to-follow plots • popular topics
For children who are ready to read on their own.

Reading Paragraphs   Grades 2–3
• challenging vocabulary • short paragraphs • exciting stories
For newly independent readers who read simple sentences with confidence.

Ready for Chapters   Grades 2–4
• chapters • longer paragraphs • full-color art
For children who want to take the plunge into chapter books but still like colorful pictures.

STEP INTO READING® is designed to give every child a successful reading experience. The grade levels are only guides. Children can progress through the steps at their own speed, developing confidence in their reading, no matter what their grade.

Remember, a lifetime love of reading starts with a single step!

Thomas the Tank Engine & Friends ™ CREATED BY BR*Brtt*T ALLCROFT

Based on the Railway Series by the Reverend W Awdry
© 2012, 2017 Gullane (Thomas) LLC. Thomas the Tank Engine & Friends
and Thomas & Friends are trademarks of Gullane (Thomas) Limited.
Thomas the Tank Engine & Friends and Design Is Reg. U.S. Pat. & Tm. Off.
© 2017 HIT Entertainment Limited.

Visit us on the Web!
StepIntoReading.com
randomhousekids.com
www.thomasandfriends.com

ISBN 978-1-5247-1657-8 (trade) — ISBN 978-1-5247-1658-5 (lib. bdg.)

Printed in the United States of America
10 9 8 7 6 5 4 3 2 1

HIT entertainment

THOMAS
& FRIENDS™

THOMAS
AND THE PIGLETS

Based on the Railway Series by the Reverend W Awdry

Random House 🏠 New York

Thomas the Tank Engine
liked to visit
Farmer Trotter's farm.

He loved seeing the pigs.

Oink, oink!

The farmer had news.
One of his pigs was
going to have piglets!

He asked Thomas
to bring some straw
from the next farm.
The straw would make
a cozy bed for the piglets!

But Thomas also wanted
to bring a gift
for the piglets.

What else could he bring?

Thomas passed Percy.
He was getting
milk at the Dairy.

Thomas asked for some
milk for the piglets.
Percy was glad
to share.

Then Thomas saw James
at the apple farm.
He was getting apples.

Thomas asked for apples
for the piglets.
James was glad
to share.

Next Thomas saw
some children
picking chestnuts.

Thomas asked if he
could take some nuts
for the piglets.
The children were glad
to share.

At last Thomas got
to the next farm.
Now he would get
straw for the piglets.

But Thomas did not have
room for the straw!
His truck was full of
milk, apples,
and nuts.

Thomas sped back
to Trotter's farm.
He dropped off the
milk, apples,
and nuts.

Farmer Trotter told Thomas
to rush back
with the straw.
The piglets would be
born soon!

Soon Thomas came back with lots of soft straw. He was just in time!

The farmer opened
the barn door.

There were
the new piglets!
They were very sleepy.

Farmer Trotter put the
straw on the ground.
It was soft and warm.
The piglets lay down
and fell asleep.

Farmer Trotter
thanked Thomas.
He even named one
of the piglets Thomas!
Hooray!